ω
9.16

JE -- 12

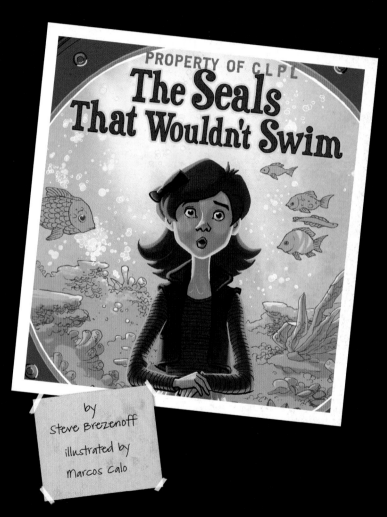
PROPERTY OF C L P L

# The Seals That Wouldn't Swim

by
Steve Brezenoff

illustrated by
Marcos Calo

STONE ARCH BOOKS
a capstone imprint

r Samantha Archer,

Field Trip Mysteries are published by Stone Arch Books
A Capstone Imprint
151 Good Counsel Drive, P.O. Box 669
Mankato, Minnesota 56002
www.capstonepub.com

Library of Congress Cataloging-in-Publication Data
Brezenoff, Steven.
  The seals that wouldn't swim / by Steve Brezenoff ;
illustrated by Marcos Calo.
      p. cm. --  (Field trip mysteries)
  ISBN-13: 978-1-4342-3225-0 (library binding)
  ISBN-10: 1-4342-3225-5 (library binding)
  ISBN-13: 978-1-4342-3428-5 (pbk.)
  ISBN-10: 1-4342-3428-2 (pbk.)
  1.  Seals (Animals)--Juvenile fiction. 2.  Aquariums--
Juvenile fiction. 3.  School field trips--Juvenile fiction. 4.
Animal welfare--Juvenile fiction. 5.  Animal rights activists-
-Juvenile fiction. 6.  Detective and mystery stories. [1.
Mystery and detective stories. 2. Seals (Animals)--Fiction.
3. Aquariums--Fiction. 4. School field trips--Fiction. 5.
Animals--Treatment--Fiction.]  I. Calo, Marcos, ill. II.
Title. III. Title: Seals that would not swim. IV. Series:
Brezenoff, Steven. Field trip mysteries.
  PZ7.B7576Se 2011                          2011002174
  813.6--dc22

Art Director/Graphic Designer: Kay Fraser

Summary: On a science class trip to the
aquarium, Catalina "Cat" Duran and her friends
discover that two of the seals have been
drugged and investigate to discover the person
responsible.

Printed in the United States of America in Stevens Point,
Wisconsin.
032011
                      006111WZF11

# TABLE OF CONTENTS

**Catalina Duran**

A.K.A: Cat

D.O.B: February 15th

POSITION: 6th Grade

**INTERESTS:**

Animals, being "green", field trips

**KNOWN ASSOCIATES:**

Archer, Samantha; Garrison, Edward; and Shoo, James. *Are these students spending too much time together?*

**NOTES:**

Catalina is well liked by most of her teachers and fellow students. *Sounds like a troublemaker.*

## UNDERWATER

As we entered the tunnel,
my friend Egg said,
"This is amazing.
Isn't it, Cat?"

I nodded. The tunnel was made completely of glass, and it was the entrance to the City Aquarium. The moment we entered, we were surrounded by underwater creatures of all shapes, sizes, and colors.

"It is pretty cool," our friend Sam said.

"I can't believe the glass doesn't break," Gum said. Gum was the fourth member of our group. "Imagine if it did!"

"Oh, Gum," I said. "Stop it."

Just then, a long, mean-looking shark swam right over us. I shrieked.

Gum laughed. "Ooh," he said, poking my shoulder. "I sure hope the glass doesn't break."

"Okay, okay," I said. I felt myself turning red. "So the shark scared me. Sharks are scary."

"Listen up, everyone!" Mr. Neff, our science teacher, called from the front. Our sixth-grade class was on a science field trip. And so far, it was really cool.

"We're about to enter the aquarium," Mr. Neff went on when the class was quiet. "While we're inside, you are to listen to three people very closely. First, our assistant teacher from the local college, Winnie Hucker," Mr. Neff said.

A tall young woman we'd all seen in science class jogged over from deeper in the tunnel.

She stopped next to Mr. Neff. "Um, hi," she said. She blushed. "My name is Wendy Zucker, actually."

"Oh, excuse me," Mr. Neff said. "You're right. Of course."

He often has trouble with names. For three weeks in September, he called me Mouse instead of Cat.

"Next, please keep an ear out for Anton's father, Mr. Gunnut," Mr. Neff said.

"Gutman," Anton's dad shouted from behind us. "My name is Mr. Gutman, not Gunnut."

"Yes, of course," Mr. Neff said. "Now, let's all move quietly and calmly into the aquarium itself."

He turned around and started walking quickly through the tunnel.

My friends and I glanced at each other.

"Um, Mr. Neff?" Sam called out. She put up her hand.

"Yes, what is it, Samantha?" he replied.

"Who is the third person we should listen to?" Sam asked.

Mr. Neff frowned. Then he said, "Me, of course."

The class laughed. Then Mr. Neff led us farther into the tunnel, curving through the water.

# CHAPTER TWO

# CRAZINESS

Mr. Neff and the rest of the class moved through quickly, but I wanted to see the animals. Soon I was far behind everyone else with the assistant teacher, Wendy.

"You must love animals as much as I do," Wendy said to me.

"I sure do," I said. "I adore animals."

Wendy smiled. "I wasn't that excited about this trip," she said. "But at least I'll have good company: another animal lover!"

Wendy and I stepped into the bright main room of the aquarium.

As soon as we did, we stopped short. I felt Wendy's hand grab my shoulder.

"Oh, my," she said. "What's this all about?"

The place was a madhouse.

Aquarium workers and visitors were standing around trying to shout over one another.

In the middle of the huge group were a very tall man and a very tall woman. The man was waving his arms, trying to calm everyone down.

I ducked away from Wendy and quickly found Egg, Sam, and Gum near the edge of the crowd.

All three of my friends were standing there, staring around the room. Sam narrowed her eyes as she gazed as the crowd. I knew right away what she was thinking.

Every time we go on a field trip, Sam is sure that it's going to turn into a mystery we need to solve.

Of course, she's usually right. For some reason, mysteries seem to follow us.

"Is there trouble?" I asked.

"There you are," Egg said. "Yeah, it sure looks like trouble."

Gum rolled his eyes. "These two always think it's trouble," he told me.

Sam glared at him. "The first seal show is canceled," she said. "We don't know why yet, but we're going to find out."

"Do you think it's foul play?" I asked.

"I'd bet anything," Sam said. She squinted at me and touched the tip of her nose. Then she went back to staring at the crowd.

"Everyone, please calm down," cried out the man in the middle. "The second show will go on as scheduled. Tickets will be for sale at the ticket window right away. If you have tickets already, you can exchange them — at the window!"

The crowd got quiet, and everyone headed for the ticket window.

Most of our classmates were standing next to Mr. Neff. My friends and I, though, hung around the tall man and tall woman.

As most of the other people left, we realized that a third person was with the two tall people. A much shorter man, who had a skinny mustache.

"Do you know how much this is going to cost the aquarium?" the tall man asked.

The woman just sneered at him and rolled her eyes.

"A lot, that's how much," the tall man went on. "We need these shows to keep the aquarium afloat. Pardon the pun."

"Ha!" the woman said. "Mr. Low, it's no wonder the seals won't wake up to perform."

Sam elbowed me. "Now we know why the show was canceled," she whispered. I nodded.

"The way you schedule these shows," the woman went on, "they're exhausted. They work too hard!"

"Darn it, Ms. Dyer," Mr. Low said. "What do you want me to do? The aquarium needs the money." Then he stormed off.

Ms. Dyer and the shorter man stood there quietly for a moment. Then the shorter man said, "I don't know what you're complaining about. At least you have a show."

"Oh, stop it, Mr. Shortz," Ms. Dyer said. "No one ever bought tickets to your goldfish show. It had to be canceled."

Ms. Dyer started to walk away.

Just then, two people in aquarium uniforms came running over.

"Ms. Dyer!" one of them shouted.

"Yes, what is it?" she asked, frowning. "Is everything okay with my seals?"

The two workers shook their heads. "I'm afraid they're not just sleeping," one of them said. "Someone gave them a tranquilizer. They've been drugged!"

# DRUGGED

"So, someone slipped the seals a mickey," Sam said. We were sitting on a bench outside, near the stingray tanks. Sam leaned back and wiggled a toothpick between her teeth.

"Someone did what?" Gum asked.

"Slipped them a mickey," Egg said. "I'm pretty sure she means someone gave them a drug to make them sleep, like the aquarium worker said."

"Ah," Gum said.

He and I nodded. Usually at least one of us understood Sam's weird lingo. Sometimes no one did, so we often just shrugged and moved on. Sam didn't seem to care one way or the other.

"The question is, who did it?" Sam asked. She sighed. "I guess it's up to us to find out."

Gum rolled his eyes. "Come on, not this time," he said. "Honestly. Can't we just try to enjoy this field trip without trying to solve a crime?"

Mr. Low, the aquarium director, walked past then. He was talking on his cell phone, and he seemed very frazzled.

"Please, send Detective Jones as soon as possible," he snapped into his cell phone. "Right away. Faster than right away. Immediately!"

I don't think he knew we were sitting there, though, because then Mr. Low added, "And keep it quiet! I don't want to make this a big scene. I mean it this time. Please, keep it quiet!"

He hung up, slipped his phone into his pants pocket, and walked on.

"See that?" Gum said. "The cops will handle it. Let's forget about it, okay? Now come on. Let's check out the aquarium."

"I think I'm with Gum, guys," Egg said. He tapped his camera. "I don't want to miss a bunch of great shots of all these colorful fish while we hunt for a seal-drugger."

I couldn't believe what I was hearing! These were my best friends, and they were turning down an important case.

I jumped up from the bench and stomped my feet.

"We must solve this case," I said. "We must do it. For the seals! Don't let me down, guys. Please?"

Sam was at my side in an instant. "I'm in," she said. I knew she would be. She'd never turn down a case.

Gum looked at me. "All right, I'll solve it for you right now," he said. "And I don't even have to get up. It was Anton Gutman."

I rolled
my eyes,
and so did Sam.

"You always say that," Sam said. "And you're never right."

I nodded. "It's true," I said.

"This time, I'm sure," Gum said. "Do you know why people kill seals, Cat?"

"Yes," I said. "For their fur."

"Exactly," Gum said. Then he nodded at something behind me and Sam. "Well, get a load of that coat that Anton's dad is wearing."

Sam and I turned to look. There was Mr. Gutman. I couldn't believe I hadn't noticed it before. Mr. Gutman was wearing a sleek, expensive-looking fur coat.

Seal.

"For you, Cat," Egg said, "we'll crack this case."

I sniffed and thanked him. Sam had an arm around me, and Gum was patting my head. "There, there," he said as I cried.

I couldn't believe Mr. Gutman was wearing a fur coat. The thought of those poor seals being turned into a coat turned my stomach, and I'd burst into tears. Luckily my friends were with me.

We spent a long time after that hanging around the entrance to the seal show. Mr. Neff had purchased our class tickets for the afternoon show, so for now the whole class was spread out in the aquarium.

Wendy checked in on us from time to time, but as long as we were all being good, we could do whatever we wanted. We wanted to hang out and talk about the case, so that's what we did. Of course, we were also on a stakeout.

"I have a lot of photos here," Egg said just before lunch came around. "I don't know if there are any clues, though."

"That's okay," Sam said. "Let's break the stakeout until after lunch, huh?"

She patted my shoulder and I nodded slowly.

"All right. I guess we might as well give up for a while," I said. "We're not getting anything done here."

Wendy came by just then. She smiled at me. "Did you hear the news?" she asked us. "One of the drugged seals is awake and healthy now. They're going to put on a free noon show with just one seal."

"Oh, I'm so glad she's okay!" I said. I really was. Some people might think it's dumb to worry about a seal, but I love all animals.

Wendy smiled. "I'll go tell everyone else the good news," she said. "See you guys soon." Then she hurried away.

"Hey, wait a minute," Gum said. "I am not missing lunch to watch a one-seal show. That is so lame."

I was about to insist — or at least offer to sneak a sandwich in — when Mr. Low came stomping past toward the seal show entrance.

Ms. Dyer was right on his heels, and Mr. Shortz was right behind her. None of them looked happy.

My friends and I quieted down so we could hear what they were saying.

"Drop it, Ms. Dyer," Mr. Low said. He didn't stop walking. In fact, it kind of looked like he was speeding up. His long legs started moving faster and faster.

"I will not drop it, Mr. Low," Ms. Dyer said, hurrying along behind him. "I won't drop it, in fact, until you agree to drop two shows from the seals' schedule. They are overworked. Drugs or not, these seals need a break!"

"You can replace the shows with my new flounder show," Mr. Shortz said. "It's fantastic."

Mr. Low stopped and spun to face the two workers following him. "That is enough," he said. "Unless you want to be the one to pick which workers to fire — and fire them — to make up the money we'd lose by canceling those shows, there will be no changes to the schedule."

Ms. Dyer didn't say anything. Neither did Mr. Shortz.

Mr. Low stared Ms. Dyer down for a moment. Then he nodded, turned, and stormed into the seal show area, out of sight.

Ms. Dyer stood there, frowning. Mr. Shortz just tried to smile.

I tapped Sam on the shoulder. "What about Ms. Dyer?" I said. "She sure is mad about how often the seals have to perform. She must fight about it with Mr. Low all the time."

"But why would she want to hurt the seals?" Egg said. "It seems like she really cares about them."

"They're not hurt," I said. "I mean, as far as we know, they're not in any danger. Maybe this was her way of protecting them."

A moment later, Mr. Low came charging out of the seal show area.

"Security," he said. He said it first in a whisper and then began to shout. Two security guards jogged over to him. My friends and I ran over there too, and got as close as we could.

"Two seals have gone missing," Mr. Low whispered to the security guards. "Polhaus and Dundy have been seal-napped!"

"Okay, everyone, try to stay calm," Gum said.

We'd moved away from the craziness near the seal show area and were walking toward the snack bar.

Wendy had shown up after the security guards were called over. She told us to meet the rest of the class for lunch.

"The seals might not have been harmed," Gum said. "They're probably fine."

I nodded.

I tried as hard as I could to imagine the seals in a big tub someplace, very safe. But images of Mr. Gutman's fur coat kept pushing their way into my brain.

"If Anton Gutman had anything to do with this . . ." I said. I narrowed my eyes. "Grrr . . ."

Pardon my anger. They call me Cat. I prefer to think of myself as a kitten, but when I think about someone hurting animals, I'm more like a lioness!

"Settle down, Cat," Sam said. "Let's stick to the facts. Like Gum said, as far as we know, the seals are just missing. They are probably perfectly safe."

"Which means it could be Ms. Dyer, like you said," Egg added.

Suddenly I spotted Ms. Dyer. She was standing just outside of the snack area, facing away from us. "It's time to find out," I said.

I shook my hair and nodded firmly. "Let's go," I said.

Then I started walking with as much confidence as I could. I was ready to make her confess.

As I got closer, though, all my confidence fell away. I wasn't losing my nerve. I had just noticed that Ms. Dyer was hunched over a little. Her shoulders were shaking.

*Oh, she's crying,* I thought.

I stopped walking. Sam bumped into my back.

"What gives, Cat?" she said, annoyed.

"Um, nothing," I said. "Stay here."

Without my friends, I walked over to Ms. Dyer and put a hand on her shoulder.

"Are you okay?" I asked her.

She was startled. Quickly, she patted her eyes with a tissue and then turned to me. She was smiling a little.

"Oh, it's the missing seals," she said. "I care about them so much. You see, I've raised them up from when they were puppies."

"I'm sorry," I said. "You must be very worried about them."

She nodded. "I am," she said. Then she patted my hand.

I guess she noticed I looked sad and worried too. "But don't you worry, dear," she said. "We'll find them."

I gave her a weak smile and headed back to my friends.

"Change of plans," I told them. "She didn't do it."

"What are you talking about?" Egg asked. "She's our biggest suspect."

"Nope. Not anymore," I said. "Uh, I think . . . uh . . . well . . . um . . ." I quickly looked around, hoping to think of a new idea.

Just then, Anton and his dad arrived in the snack area.

"Oh, Mr. Gutman," I said, nodding in his direction. "It's got to be him. That seal coat? That bad attitude? I think Gum is right on the money this time. It's Mr. Gutman. For sure. Let's go question him. Come on! Follow me! Let's crack this case!"

"Whoa," Egg said.

"Are you serious?" Sam asked. "You're the one who thought it was Ms. Dyer."

Gum smiled and nodded. "Nice. Cat agrees with me," he said. "And she's the **smartest one here.**"

"Oh, shush," Sam said. She rolled her eyes. Then she turned and faced Mr. Gutman as he sat down at a nearby table. "Okay, let's do this."

# CHAPTER SIX

## SAVING SEATS

As we reached Mr. Gutman, the rest of our class, Mr. Neff, and Wendy all showed up too. Everyone started claiming tables.

I noticed Ms. Dyer quickly running away from the rest of us. I guess she was embarrassed.

Sam elbowed me. "Look at her. Running off," she said. "Feeling guilty, I bet."

"What do you want?" Mr. Gutman said suddenly.

My friends and I jumped, but nobody said anything. "You're standing around my table staring at me. What do you want?" he asked again.

"Um, may we sit here?" I said, smiling as big as I could.

He scratched his chin and took off his coat. "Er, I suppose," he said. Then he put the coat down on his seat, next to Anton's bag. "Watch the table. You four can go get your food after my son and I get back."

He got up from the table and hurried over to the snack counter. Anton was already there waiting for him. We heard Anton whine loudly.

"We're sitting with the dorks?" he groaned.

"Okay," Sam said. "Let's look through their stuff."

Gum nodded, and the two of them started pawing at the Gutmans' things.

"What are you doing?" Wendy said, practically shrieking as she walked up to the table.

"Um, we're just watching Mr. Gutman's things for him," I said quickly. "He and Anton went to get their lunches."

She gave me a long look. "Mm-hm," she said. "Okay."

Wendy looked around at the snack area. There were very few seats left. She put her bag down next to me. "Do you mind if I sit with you?" she asked.

I smiled and nodded. "Of course not!" I said. "We'll watch your bag for you, too."

"Thanks," Wendy said. Then she went off to get her lunch.

"Why does everyone get to order lunch before us?" Gum asked. He rubbed his stomach. "This is totally unfair," he muttered.

"Quiet," Sam said. "This way we can check out their stuff and see if they're suspects."

"Wendy's stuff?" I asked. "Wendy isn't a suspect at all."

"Everyone's a suspect," Sam said, squinting. She can be pretty weird sometimes.

"This is weird," Gum said. He was looking at some stuff on Mr. Gutman's chair. "What's 'acrylic' mean?"

"Man-made," I said. "Like, in painting, acrylic means chemical paints, instead of oils. So, like, fake."

"Well, then this is fake fur," Gum said, holding up Mr. Gutman's coat collar. "See?"

The tag read,
"100%
Acrylic.
All man-made
material."

"Wow," I said. "I'm shocked."

Sam nodded. "Me too," she said. "He doesn't seem like the type to wear fake anything."

"Hey, put that down," Mr. Gutman shouted. He was standing a few feet from us, holding a big cardboard tray of hot dogs and sodas. Anton was right behind him, sneering.

Gum quickly dropped the collar and the coat fell back onto the seat.

"I'm — I'm sorry, Mr. Gutman," I said. "I really am." I felt so ashamed.

Mr. Gutman put the tray down on the table. "What were you kids doing?" he asked me.

I looked at my hands. "We were just checking the tag," I said. "We wanted to see if . . . what kind of fur . . ."

Mr. Gutman's face went soft. He turned to his son, who was also carrying a load of hot dogs and sodas.

"Anton," Mr. Gutman said. "Put those down on the table and go get us some straws."

Anton rolled his eyes, but he put everything down and headed back toward the stand.

Mr. Gutman called after him, "And some mustard packets. And napkins. Plenty of napkins."

Mr. Gutman waited until Anton was out of earshot. Then he put an arm around my shoulder. "What's this about, young lady?" he asked.

"Those seals," I said. "I'm worried about them, and your coat looks like seal fur."

Mr. Gutman's face turned white. He nodded slowly, and his eyes got wet. "I'd never," he said. "I would never hurt a poor helpless animal."

"You wouldn't?" I asked.

I glanced at my friends.

Egg lowered his camera and frowned.

Sam gave me a very confused look.

Gum looked like he might explode with laughter. But he managed to hold it in.

I looked back at Anton's dad. "You like animals?" I asked quietly.

Mr. Gutman shook his head. "Those poor seals," he said. Then he really started crying.

I patted his knee. "There, there," I said. "I'm sorry we thought it might be you, Mr. Gutman."

"Do you think they'll find those poor seals?" he asked.

"I'm sure they will," I said. "My friends and I are going to help however we can. Don't worry. We'll figure this one out."

Mr. Gutman's face became hopeful and bright. "You will?" he said. "For real? Are you sure?"

I nodded and smiled and patted his hand. "We sure will," I said.

"Hey, Dad," Anton called. He was walking toward us with the stuff his dad had asked for. Including about three hundred napkins. "These were all the napkins I could find. Is it enough?"

Mr. Gutman sat up suddenly and wiped his eyes. "Yes, yes," he said to his son. He didn't look at him, though. "That's fine. Let's eat."

"Finally," Gum said.

I looked at the food on the table. There must have been twelve hot dogs and sodas there, not to mention the huge bucket of fries.

"Oh, and um," Mr. Gutman said, waving over the food. "I bought lunch for the table. Obviously."

I smiled at him. He winked at me. Then the six of us ate lunch.

After we ate, the Gutmans headed off to the bathroom. Wendy, meanwhile, still hadn't gotten back to the table with her lunch. I didn't see her in line, either.

"Where do you think the TA ran off to?" Gum said. He carefully leaned over her bag and peeked inside.

"Hey," I said, knocking his hand away. "She is not a suspect."

"Sam says everyone is," Gum said.

He reached for the bag again, and I tried to pull it away. Instead, we both tugged it and it flew off the chair. Everything spilled all over.

"Great," I said, getting up. "Now look what you did."

Egg snapped a few pictures of the little mess Gum and I had made. "Ooh, she has a really cool phone," he said.

I got up to repack Wendy's bag, but Gum grabbed the phone before I could reach it. "I want one of these," he said. "I hear the games are amazing."

"The camera's great too," Egg said. He put his hand out. "Let me see it."

"Both of you, knock it off," I said. I tried to grab Wendy's phone from Gum. "That's not yours."

"Relax," Gum said. "I just want to try it out. Let's see. . . ."

He turned his back to me to box me out. Then he started pressing buttons and tapping the screen. Soon a web browser popped up. On the screen was a picture of a seal and a load of text.

"Hey, look at this," Gum said. We stopped struggling, and the four of us gathered around the phone.

"Is that a seal?" I asked.

Gum nodded. "Sure is," he said. "And this is an animal rights page."

Sam grabbed the phone. "Let me see," she said. She quickly scanned the page. "It's instructions to liberate the seals here. From someone called 'Freedom Kid.'"

"Must be an animal rights person," Egg said. "A secret organization and a code name and instructions for being a criminal."

Sam held up the phone in front of my face. "See?" she said. "I told you she was a suspect."

I plopped down on the bench at the table. "I can't believe it," I said. "She seemed so nice."

Gum patted my shoulder. "And she's a criminal," he said. "While Mr. Gutman is actually a very nice man."

"A total softie," Egg said.

"Just goes to show you," Sam said.

"Show you what?" I asked.

She sat down next to me.

"Sometimes, people surprise you," she said.

"I never expected to find out that a Gutman was a nice person," Gum said. "That's pretty much the surprise of this trip, for me, anyway."

"So what do we do now?" I asked, looking up at my friends. "How do we help save the seals?"

Egg sighed. "I'll find Mr. Neff," he said. "He can take it from here."

Just then, I saw Wendy walk around a corner. She headed down a hallway, going toward the exhibits.

I jumped up to follow her. When I turned the corner, I saw that she'd stopped. She was leaning against a wall, like she was waiting for someone.

When I saw her, I realized how angry I was. Not just angry, but hurt.

I'd thought she was sweet, just like me. But she was breaking the law, kidnapping seals, maybe putting them in danger.

I was furious.

"Wendy!" I shouted. I don't think she heard me. She stood there next to the wall and took a sip from the soda she was carrying.

But my friends heard me. I stomped toward her. Gum, Sam, and Egg ran up, and stomped right alongside me.

"Slow down," Sam hissed at my ear. "Maybe we should wait. We can let security handle this."

"Or the cops," Gum said. "They're around here somewhere. Mr. Low called them, remember?"

I shook my head. "No way," I said. "I'm dealing with Wendy."

That time, she heard me. Wendy smiled at me, but she could tell I was angry. She still didn't know why, though.

I held up her bag as I strode toward her.

"Where are they?" I shouted at her. She was still a few yards away.

As I got closer, I saw Wendy's eyes darting around nervously. "Where are who?" she said. "The rest of your class? They're mostly still having lunch, silly."

She chuckled nervously and took another sip from her soda.

"You know who I mean," I said. I stopped right in front of her and shoved her bag into her chest. She dropped her soda and grabbed the bag. "The seals."

"The seals?" Wendy said. She put a hand on my shoulder. "I'm sure the police will find them, sweetie."

I shook her off. Then I spotted Ms. Dyer over Wendy's shoulder a few feet away. I had created a bit of a scene, and Ms. Dyer was watching.

I decided to talk even louder.

"You know what I'm talking about," I said. "You kidnapped the seals. Or should I say, liberated them?"

Egg was at my side, and he held up his camera. He had snapped a photo of the email Gum had found. He showed it to Wendy.

Wendy's face turned white.

"Go ahead and deny it," Sam said. She leaned casually against the wall. "I could use a good laugh."

When I looked over, Ms. Dyer had disappeared. Seconds later, she was next to us, and beside her were Mr. Low and Detective Jones from the police.

"What is going on here?" the detective said.

"See for yourself," Egg said. He handed the detective his camera and showed him how to zoom in on the photo of Wendy's email.

"I see," the detective said. "This is from your email?" he asked, looking at Wendy.

She looked at her feet and nodded. "They were mistreated here," she said. "They'll be happier where they are."

"And where
is that,
exactly?"
the detective asked.

But Wendy didn't answer. She just stared at her feet.

"You'd better answer him, young lady," Ms. Dyer said. She looked angrier than I felt. "If they're in any danger . . ."

I grabbed Wendy's bag and fished around for the phone. I handed it to the detective. "Here," I said.

Wendy reached for it, but I held it away from her.

"Hey, give that to me!" she said.

"Wendy had clear instructions from someone else," I said. "It's all in the email. It might say where she put them."

The detective clicked around in Wendy's phone. We all watched his eyes as he quickly read. "Redding Lake," he said. "That's a two-minute drive from here."

"Redding Lake?!" Ms. Dyer said. "You fool. There are no fish in there. No food! It's a man-made lake. It's fake!"

"An *acrylic* lake," Gum said.

I sighed.

Everyone turned to him and stared for a moment.

I cleared my throat. "Well?" I said.

"Oh, right," Mr. Low said. He waved at a couple of uniformed employees nearby. "Get the van, boys. We're going to Redding Lake to collect Polhaus and Dundy."

A few hours later, the whole class gathered at the seal show. All three seals were healthy and ready to perform.

"Before we begin," Mr. Low announced, "a quick change to the schedule. There will now be only two seal shows per day. One in the morning, one in the afternoon."

"Huh," Gum said quietly. "How will they make up the lost funds?"

I shrugged.

"This is possible thanks to an anonymous donation from a very generous visitor," Mr. Low said.

I scanned the crowd and saw Mr. Gutman sitting with Anton near the back. He saw me and winked.

The show began.

The seals were really amazing. They jumped from the water. They jumped through hoops. They even seemed to tell jokes with their barks and clapping.

We had a great time.

As we got on the bus at the end of the day, we were feeling pretty good. The four of us piled into the two back seats.

Sam turned to Gum. "I just have one question," she said.

"What's that?" Gum asked.

He blew a big bubble. It smelled like cherry cola.

"'Acrylic lake'?" Sam asked.

Egg and I laughed and laughed.

"What?" Gum said, looking at the three of us. "What did I say?"

## literary news

# MYSTERIOUS WRITER REVEALED!

Steve Brezenoff lives in St. Paul, Minnesota, with his wife, Beth, their son, Sam, and their small, smelly dog, Harry. Besides writing books, he enjoys playing video games, riding his bicycle, and helping middle-school students work on their writing skills. Steve's ideas almost always come to him in his dreams, so he does his best writing in his pajamas.

## arts & entertainment

# ARTIST IS KEY TO SOLVING MYSTERY, SAY POLICE

Marcos Calo lives happily in A Coruña, Spain, with his wife, Patricia (who is also an illustrator), and their daughter, Claudia. When Marcos and Patricia aren't drawing, they like to go on long walks by the sea. They also watch a lot of films and eat Nutella sandwiches. Yum!

# A Detective's Dictionary

**acrylic** (uh-KRIL-ik)—a chemical substance used to make fibers and paints

**aquarium** (uh-KWAIR-ee-uhm)—a special building that showcases different species that live in water

**assistant** (uh-SISS-tuhnt)—a person who helps someone else do a job

**canceled** (KAN-suhld)—stopped from happening

**confidence** (KON-fuh-duhnss)—the belief that you will succeed

**instructions** (in-STRUHK-shuhnz)—directions on how to do something

**liberate** (LIB-uh-rayt)—set free

**organization** (or-guh-nuh-ZAY-shuhn)—people joined together for a particular purpose

**overworked** (oh-vur-WURKD)—worked too hard or too much

**scheduled** (SKEJ-uld)—planned

**tranquilizer** (TRANG-kwul-i-zur)—a drug that makes someone feel calm and peaceful or unable to move

Cat Duran
6th Grade

## Animal Rights

On our field trip to the aquarium, our assistant teacher was arrested because she illegally released the seals. She is involved with an animal rights group. The group she belonged to used unlawful techniques to make their opinions known. However, there are other, legal ways to support animal rights.

The most famous and largest animal rights group is PETA. PETA stands for People for the Ethical Treatment of Animals. With more than two million members worldwide, PETA is often in the news for making commercials or other advertisements urging people to take care of animals. But they also work to educate people on animal cruelty.

Animal cruelty can affect many different areas of life. Some people who are concerned about animal cruelty choose to not eat meat. They are called vegetarians. People who eat no red meat or poultry, but do eat fish, are called pescetarians. And people who consume no animal products at all – not even things like honey and eggs – are called vegans. People may choose to not wear clothing made from animal products like leather or wool, and they may choose to not use products that are tested on animals, like some cosmetics and bath products.

The lives of animals affect our own lives, and we can help them!

Great job, Puppy! You've given me a lot to think about. Maybe I'll try being a vegetarian for a few days. –Mr. Neff

# FURTHER INVESTIGATIONS

CASE #FTM10CAQ

1. In this book, Mr. Neff's science class (including me) went on a field trip. What field trips have you gone on? Which one was your favorite, and why?

2. What could Wendy have done to help the animals besides "liberating" them?

3. Who else could have been a suspect in this mystery?

# IN YOUR OWN DETECTIVE'S NOTEBOOK . . .

1. Wendy and I are passionate about animal rights. What is something that you care about a lot? What do you do to support that effort?

2. Have you ever been to an aquarium? What was the coolest thing you saw there? If you've never been to one, what kind of animal would you like to see at an aquarium?

3. This book is a mystery story. Write your own mystery story!

# THEY SOLVE CRIMES,
## CATCH CROOKS,
## CRACK CODES,
## ...AND RIDE THE BUS BACK TO
### SCHOOL AFTERWARD.

Meet Egg, Gum, Sam, and Cat. Four sixth-grade detectives and best friends. Wherever field trips take them, mysteries aren't far behind!

FIELD TRIP MYSTERIES

The Cave That Shouldn't Collapse

by Steve Brezenoff

Illustrated by Marcos Calo

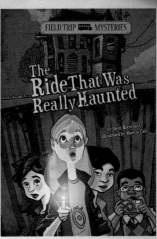

FIELD TRIP MYSTERIES

The Ride That Was Really Haunted

by Steve Brezenoff

Illustrated by Marcos Calo

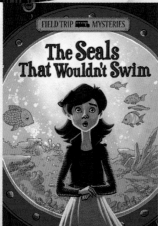

FIELD TRIP MYSTERIES

The Seals That Wouldn't Swim

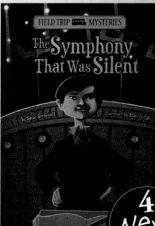

FIELD TRIP MYSTERIES

The Symphony That Was Silent

by Steve Brezenoff

Illustrated by Marcos Calo

4 NEW Mysteries